GLAMORINA

TIARRA RUNS FOR PRESIDENT

Written by
Nicole Jackson

Illustrated by
Rena Chen

ISBN: 9781694656414

First printing, 2019.

Instagram: GlamorinaBooks

Facebook: Glamorina

You Go Glamorina

!

_____

(Sign your name here)

"Crown? Check.

Science experiment? Check.

Tutu? Check.

Math assignment? Check.

Speech? Check, check, and check!"

"Tiarra, here are your **election** cupcakes," Maman says.

"Ready family? 3-2-1 **GLAMORINA**!"

"GLAMORINA!" we all shout back.

I smile. Whenever my family is **passionate** about something, we count down and cheer. We are passionate about being a Glamorina, which means you can be both girly and strong.

"I believe in you Miss **President**," Papa says.

And with that, I feel ready for today's election!

At school, I start passing my cupcakes out right away.

"A cupcake for you, a cupcake for you. Don't forget to vote for me today."

A cupcake is suddenly snatched from the corner of my tray, followed by a smug, unwelcomed voice.

"You're not going to win."

My classmate Jasper, who is also running for class president, is slowly peeling the cupcake wrapper away.

"You're a girl."

I pretend not to hear.

"There are barely any girl presidents," he says, his mouth dripping with ballerina sparkles. "Besides, not only are you a girl, but you're the girliest of girls! A Glamorina! All you do is talk about outfits and sparkles and kittens … and that tutu you always wear! Nobody will take you seriously, let alone vote for you as president."

I stand firm to let Jasper know that his words don't discourage me. "Jasper, I'm not sure if you understand what you're saying."

I turn around and see my friends Ruby, Mica, and Topaz
who saw the whole thing. My BFF, Ruby, breaks the silence.

"Forget about those mean words, Tiarra! He shouldn't make you feel bad. Besides, you would make a great president! Remember the first day of school, when you sat with me because I didn't know anyone?"

"Yeah!" says Topaz. "Or that one time I lost my favorite ball on the playground and you spent all recess looking for it with me?"

"It is so true!" exclaims Mica. "You are always thinking of ways you can help others, which is exactly why you would make a great president! There has to be a way to show everyone that Glamorinas can be president."

"Mroow, mroow, purr, purr!"

"I have an idea,

but I'll need everyone's help."

The moment is finally here—it's time for election speeches. Standing backstage, I sneak a peek at the auditorium, where my whole elementary school is listening to Jasper.

"...and that's why you should vote for me. Thank you," he says.

The crowd _____ means I'm next. I smooth out my
tutu and _____.

"Hello, fellow classmates and friends. Today, I come to you, not as a girl or a boy, but as the right person for this presidency. I want to give everyone a voice and change our school for the better." I look over and see Jasper, who's standing backstage with a mean smirk. I feel nervous, but I take a deep breath and continue anyway.

"I know people are saying that I shouldn't be president because of what I wear and the things I like, but I'm here to tell you that this stuff doesn't matter. Being a Glamorina is about being both girly and strong, which means I can wear a tutu and be president. Look!"

I watch Topaz stand up in his seat
and reveal a big, puffy tutu.
Everyone starts to giggle.

"Topaz has the highest grades in the class and wearing a tutu doesn't change that. And look at Ruby!"

"Ruby is the fastest runner at recess! And with or without a tutu, she'll still beat you at any race."

SPEECH

Ruby flexes her arms and makes a curtsy.

18

"And look at Mica! He won this year's spelling bee, and wearing a tutu doesn't stop him from learning."

19

"Glamorina,
G-L-A-M-O-R-I-N-A,
Glamorina."

"Meow,
M-E-O-W,
Meow."

"Look around! All these people are special and unique, and wearing a tutu doesn't change that! Presidents can be all shapes, sizes, colors, AND they can even wear tutus!

As a Glamorina, I know that Jasper shouldn't win just because he is a boy and I shouldn't win just because I am a girl. Whoever wins should win because they are the best person for the job. If I become your class president, I will make sure you are heard and valued, no matter what you look like or what you enjoy."

In the excitement of the moment, I yell, "3-2-1, GLAMORINA!"

The crowd goes quiet.

I try again. "3-2-1, GLAMORINA!"

"Glamorina!" A few voices trickle back at me.

"One more time," I say, and with all my might I shout,

"3-2-1, GLAMORINA!"

And just like that, the whole auditorium chants back,

"GLAMORINA, GLAMORINA, GLAMORINA!"

And guess who won!

La Fin

GLOSSARY

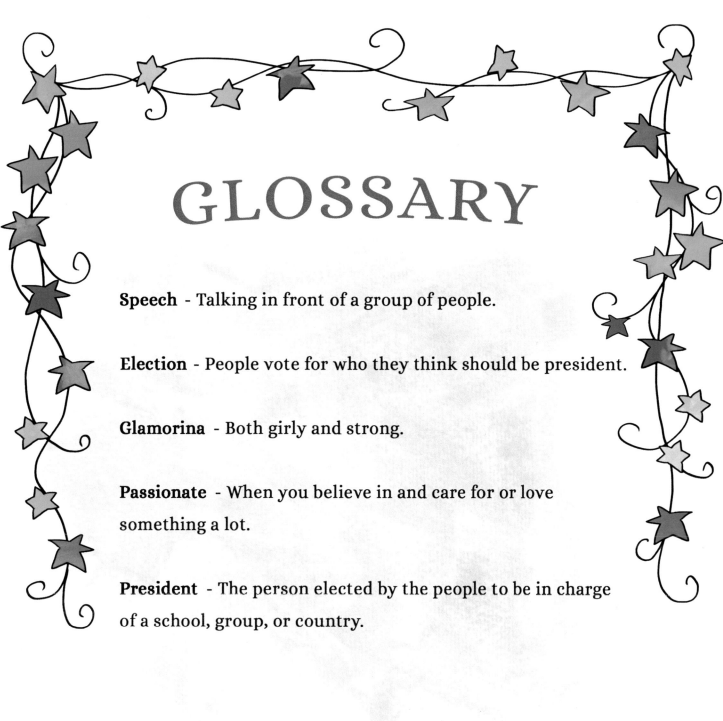

Speech - Talking in front of a group of people.

Election - People vote for who they think should be president.

Glamorina - Both girly and strong.

Passionate - When you believe in and care for or love something a lot.

President - The person elected by the people to be in charge of a school, group, or country.

Glam Up Your Glamorina!

(Color me in)

Made in United States
North Haven, CT
07 August 2022

22395154R00018